Hitched for *Life*

notionpress.com

Hitched for Life

Anchal Rana Aggarwal

notionpress.com

Notion Press

Old No. 38, New No. 6

McNichols Road, Chetpet

Chennai - 600 031

First Published by Notion Press 2015

ISBN 978-93-5206-424-3

To my husband Dheeraj and my late grandfather Thakur Ganpat Rai

Acknowledgements

I wrote short stories when I was young but I never thought that I would grow up to write a novel. Sometimes, unexpected events happen in life.

Above all I want to thank Lord Ganesha for blessing me with beautiful people. I want to thank my husband Dheeraj for being a pillar of support. Without his encouragement, I may not have written this book.

I want to thank my father-in-law, Amar Kumar Aggarwal, for letting me be me, and my brother-in-law Hemant for helping me with the technical aspects.

I also want to thank my father Dr Ravinder Singh Rana, my mother Kiran Rana, and my brother Rahul for their love and support.

My heartfelt thanks to my *mausi*, Dr Neeraj Rajan, for guiding me, and my cousin Akshima and my friends Kanika, Sonal, Maulshree, Gaurav.

Thanks to the team at Notion Press for accepting my book proposal and helping me publish it. Without them, my dreams would not have turned into reality.

And last, but not the least, thanks to my readers for choosing to read my book. Hope you all like it.

Contents

1

The Beginning

Standing in front of the mirror with the *dupatta* from my wedding outfit over my head, I wondered how I would look on my wedding day. Would I look beautiful or not? My make-up did not go well with my hairdo during my engagement ceremony. This time, I didn't want to take any chances.

I clicked pictures in my wedding attire and sent them to my girlfriends for their comments. We were a gang of four girls – Ishika, Maria, Nisha and I. We were best friends from childhood. We had studied in the same school but parted ways in college when we took up different streams of study. But our friendship was forever. We were soulmates.

"Alisha *beta*," my mom called me as she entered my room.

"Oh god! How many selfies will you take? Today's generation…!"

"Mom, just take a look at my pictures."

"Aww! My beautiful daughter. Let me ward off any evil eye from you."

"Oh come on *ma*."

I looked at the wall clock. It was 11 a.m.

"Gosh, I need to go to the parlour for my bridal dress rehearsal. I am getting late."

"Wait, I will come with you."

"Mom…"

"What?"

"Okay, let's go."

On our way in the car, my mom held my hand in hers and said, "I will miss you, *beta.*" She was getting emotional. All I could manage to say was, "I will miss you too."

For the first time in my life, I was learning to express my love for my parents. They were terrific people and I wanted to thank them for everything – for putting up with my tantrums and misbehaviour and for allowing me to marry the love of my life. I wanted to tell them how much they meant to me and how much I loved them but I could not.

Aryan and I were college mates. I didn't know how my parents would react when I told them about him. I decided to tell my mom everything after my graduation. I had dropped subtle hints earlier. I had talked a lot about Aryan to her. I had told her we were best buddies but she never once questioned me.

I remember the day I told my mom about wanting to marry Aryan.

One day, when we were chatting in the kitchen, my mom told me that a family known to her wanted to explore a possibility of a marriage alliance with our family. The boy's parents wanted to 'see' me. The boy was an orthopedic surgeon. I had no other choice than to tell her about Aryan. "Mom, Aryan and I are in a relationship. I don't see a future with any other man than him."

My mom was surprised at first and then she said, "Okay, if you want to get married to him, we will make it happen. But, before finalising anything, we will meet the family and look at Aryan's earnings. Love alone is not enough for living happily. Besides, you have to convince your father too."

"Convince dad? No way, mom. I am not going to do that. You will do that for me. Please, please, please..."

"Hmm... Okay, I will."

A few days later, the topic of matchmaking popped up again. My dad hugged me and said, "One day, my dear daughter will leave me. We will find the best groom for her."

"She has already found her groom," my mom said. I was petrified. I thought my dad would pull me up and give me one tight slap. Well, he did pull me towards him. However, instead of slapping me, he asked me, "Who is he?" I was still scared. So my mother answered. "His name is Aryan and he comes from a trading community."

"Hmm... My daughter should be happy. That's all I need," said my dad and hugged me again. My heart, which had been racing till then, bounced with happiness. I was so relieved.

To my surprise, my dad was very calm about it and said, "Aryan seems to be nice. I hope his family is nice too." I was so happy that he approved of Aryan. Mom was the one who convinced my dad. I was grateful to her. My parents did have some reservations about the fact that Aryan and I came from diverse cultures, but that was not a good enough reason to say no to our marriage.

When Aryan and I started dating, I didn't think that our relationship would last long because I had seen that many college affairs died out after college but here we were making plans for our wedding. It was destiny. We were meant to be together.

2

The Day

It was November 19. It was the D-day. I woke up feeling excited. My bed was filled with crumbs of dry *henna.* I had slept without removing the *henna* from my hands because I wanted it to leave behind a dark colour. It is said that the darker the color of *henna*, the deeper is the husband's love for the wife. Some say this is also true for the relationship between the mother-in-law and daughter-in-law. Well, I really hoped my husband's love for me would be strong and deep.

I went outside to have a look at my house. It looked so beautiful, decked up in bright yellow lights and flowers. I had never found my house so beautiful before. Finally, the lights were turned off as it was a bright morning. I felt like kissing the walls of my house. This was the place where I had spent my childhood. This was where I had formed so many memories – memories of endless love, thrashings and games.

I left my house briefly to pursue my career in dentistry. However, I came back to my cosy nest. But this time, I would be gone for good. I was getting married and I would make a new home for myself.

I was born and brought up in the hill station of Manali but I never wanted to settle down there. Having lived in the hills all my life, I craved for the hustle-bustle of city life. I guess god had heard me.

I saw the clock. It showed 7 a.m. The wedding rituals were about to begin in an hour. I made a phone call to my girlfriends who were in their hotel rooms. I asked them to come over to my room soon.

My friends were working in Delhi in the corporate sector. Only I was in the field of medicine. I would soon join them in Delhi after my wedding. I was the first one to get married among the four of us. Nisha was to get married next to the love of her life, Anuj. She was engaged to him and her wedding was in six months.

I sat on the verandah wearing a yellow suit for the *haldi* ceremony. My girls came up to me.

"You are already glowing. You don't need *haldi*," said Ishika.

"I wish I have such a glow on my face on my wedding day," said Nisha.

"Well, she is our guinea pig. She will experience married life and tell us everything about it," said Maria.

We all laughed.

The ceremony started. It began on a smooth note with everyone following the instructions of the priest. Then,suddenly Maria attacked Ishika's face from behind and smeared it with *haldi*.

Ishika was petrified. It took her a while to realise what had just happened. She then scooped out a more than a handful of *haldi* from a plate and pounced on Maria. Nisha joined her. In a matter of seconds, everyone joined them and started smearing *haldi* on each other. All my relatives, cousins and even some of the older people started playing Holi with *haldi*. There was utter chaos all over the place.

Then, one of my cousins attacked the priest from behind. My parents and I were stunned. We were worried that things were getting out of control but the priest took it in his stride and started laughing.

There was happiness and laughter all around. Everyone looked like zombies drenched in *haldi.* I wished that time stood still.

My eyes met my parents' eyes. Their eyes were a tad wet with happiness. I wanted to get up and run to them. I wanted to give them a tight hug and kiss them but I stopped myself as I didn't want to break down in front of everyone. I prayed to god that my parents remained healthy and happy forever.

3

The Night

I was getting anxious. The make-up artist was working on my face. I closed my eyes and prayed that I looked ravishing. It was not that I was insecure but I wanted to rock the day. It was my day. It was the day I had dreamt of all my life.

The make-up artist sensed my apprehension and said, "Ma'am! You please relax. Just leave it to me."

"Okay, but please don't overdo it."

"I won't, ma'am."

Just then Maria came to me and said, "Gosh! You have an acne on your forehead."

"What? Where? Oh no!"

"You are silly. If you get so tensed, these things will happen."

"Can you please hide it?" I asked the make-up artist.

"Do not worry, ma'am. I will hide it with a *bindi*."

Nisha scolded Maria for getting me worked up.

"Maria, please don't make her all panicky."

"I wish there are a few handsome guys out there," said Ishika.

"Yeah," said Nisha.

I was ready and so were my girls. I was wearing a beautiful red *lehenga* with golden sequins all over. It was very heavy. We hugged each other as a group and proceeded to the *mandap*.

Everything was perfect. Just like I had dreamt it to be. The flower arrangements, the decoration, the food, everything was perfect. I felt so serene. My parents and I didn't want the Delhi crowd to find any flaw. There they were – my parents. My dad hugged me and kissed me on my forehead.

"Oh dad! Please stop. My hairdo will get ruined."

"My angel! You look so beautiful. God bless you."

I went to the bridal room and waited to be called. After sometime, I heard the firecrackers. There were butterflies in my stomach. The *baraat* had arrived.

I looked out of the large window from my room. I saw my man dancing, making silly moves, even while seated on the horse. I was happy to see him and I laughed aloud.

After sometime, my brothers took me to the stage. This was it. I was going to be Aryan's forever.

Aryan extended his hand and held my hand tight. "I am never going to leave it," he whispered into my ears. I blushed. Aryan was the love of my life. We were college sweethearts and now we would be husband and wife.

Aryan had left his job to join his father's business. He was handsome, six feet tall, and had a wheatish complexion. He was an extrovert. We danced, laughed, posed for pictures and had the time of our lives that day. Soon, the day was over. We were married. It's strange that the day for which you have waited all your life is just a few hours affair. Everything happens so fast that it gets over.

Although I wanted to live in the city, it was hard to leave my parents. I do not understand who came up with this ridiculous rule. Teary-eyed, I left for my new home, which destiny had chosen for me.

4

My New Home

I left everything behind, my family, my friends and my house. I was ready to begin a new chapter in my life. On my way to my new house, several thoughts came rushing into my mind. I hoped I had made the right decision. I had never been to Aryan's house. I wished it was beautiful. I was getting a bit anxious.

We reached Aryan's house only by 11 p.m. I was tired. But I was welcomed in style by my mother-in-law, much like how it happened in Bollywood movies. I felt like a heroine and my tiredness vanished. My house was a new three-bedroom apartment. Having lived in a big house on the hills, I had mentally prepared myself to live in a smaller apartment. That is how people live in delhi.

I was going to live in a city where I would find big crowds wherever I went. Traffic would soon become my best friend. But I would also have neighbours who didn't even know I existed. Well, Aryan had warned me about life in a metro. Thankfully, my in-laws had been mature and understanding enough to give us our own space. They bought us a flat opposite theirs and it suited me fine.

When I entered the apartment, I saw that my mother-in-law had furnished it already. I was grateful to her for taking care of the basics but my tastes were different from hers. I found the furniture quite old. I mentally made note of the changes I would have to make.

"How do you find the new place, *beta*?" my mother-in-law asked me.

"It's lovely mom but I think the kitchen is quite small."

She smiled and said, "I agree with you but in Delhi you won't find a kitchen as big as the one in your parents' house. You will get used to it slowly."

We had dinner together and went to sleep. It was our 'first night' or should I say our 'first day' as it was well past midnight. It was not that Aryan and I had not made love before but this day was special. We were married. I loved our room. It was beautifully decorated with flowers and candles, although personally I did not like flowers on a bed. We laughed at the filmy 'set-up' as we removed the flowers from the bed.

We then drank a lot of wine. Aryan and I soon drowned in happiness and intoxication. In no time, we were asleep.

5

Sister-in-law

My younger sister-in-law Akansha woke us up in the morning. We were asked to get ready for a *pooja* but my head was throbbing from the previous night's hangover. Aryan and I had drunk quite a lot of wine. I took a pill for my headache and relaxed for some time. Aryan came to me, touched my face with his hands, looked in my eyes and said," Dear, I know that I could have done much better on our first night other than serving you wine but I promise that today will be spectacular."

I bursted out laughing on hearing this and Aryan joined me. He started cuddling me and then stopped and pulled me closer to him. He looked deep into my eyes and we kissed. I felt as if it was my first kiss. Soon we were on bed making love. Aryan then went for a bath after that and I sat quietly on my bed observing my new room. It was quite spacious and cozy but not like my room at home. I had spent so many days in that room and now left it all of a sudden. It would take some time for the new room to take that position in my heart.

I was missing home badly but I didn't tell Aryan. I felt as though there was a hole in my heart. Then my phone rang. It was my mother. Mothers had this knack of knowing how their daughters felt even if they were not in front of their girls.

"How are you, *beta*?"

"I am fine, mom. Everything is good, mom."

"Okay then. Take care."

"I hope you are fine. You must be tired."

"Yes, mom. But now, after a nice sleep I am fine."

"Okay, *beta*. I just wanted to know how you are. Take care. I will call you later."

We had only a short conversation but my heart felt so relieved. I didn't talk to my father because I knew one of us would break down.

I wore a heavy work suit and jewellary for the pooja. I was quite uncomfortable as I was not at all used to all this but this was the tradition and I was supposed to follow it. All the wedding guests left except for my older sister-in-law. After the *pooja* was over, I made *halwa* for the first time. This was a tradition. To my surprise, it turned out well and everyone liked it.

My phone kept buzzing every minute. I knew my friends were trying to reach me. But I didn't have time to check my messages or answer their calls. I was expected to be calm in front of my in-laws. I could not be distracted by phone calls or text messages.

"I have to leave for office," said Aryan.

I followed him to our room.

"You are leaving already?"

"Already? I have to go, Alisha."

"Can't you join work after two days or so?"

"Look Alisha, I have a very important meeting. I cannot miss it. Everyone in the house will help you out. If you need anything, you can ask mom. She will help you arrange your wardrobe. I will come back by evening and then we will discuss our honeymoon."

"Wow! Really?"

"Yes," said Aryan, kissing my forehead. Then he left.

I sat with everyone else in the drawing room. They were talking to each other and giggling. I felt like an intruder in the room. I was not able to find the right words to say.

"Alisha, you can go to your room and arrange your things," said my mother-in-law.

The outfit I was wearing was quite uncomfortable as it was a heavy suit with gold thread work all over. I went into my room and changed into a tracksuit.

I checked the messages on my phone.

Nisha: 'How was it?'

Maria: 'What are you doing right now?'

Ishika: 'How is your mother in law?'

Maria: 'Where the hell are you?'

Ishika: 'Give us the details, girl.'

I sent them a common reply.

'Hello guys. I am absolutely fine, but quite busy right now. I'll catch up with you later.'

The girls were disappointed. They sent me a sad smiley. But I didn't have a lot of time. I had to get my wardrobe in order.

As I was unpacking my things, Mansha, my older sister-in-law, entered the room without knocking. I did not like it at all.

"What are you doing?" she asked me, in an intimidating voice.

"I am going to organise my things."

"Gosh! You changed already? You are not supposed to do that so soon."

"Why?"

"Mom may not like it. It's your first day here. You should be dressed well."

"Yes, dressed like a showpiece with all this heavy jewellery and clothing," I muttered under my breath.

"I am not comfortable in this *didi.* I will change again once I am done with my work."

My mother-in-law heard the conversation as my sister-in-law had left the door open.

"It is absolutely fine, Alisha. All the guests have left."

I didn't say anything but my sister-in-law felt embarrassed and said, "But mom, she is not supposed to be in casual clothes."

My mother-in-law didn't answer her. Instead she said that she was going to the nearby store with Akansha and would be back soon. I could see Mansha's face boiling with rage. Without saying anything more, she left the room. In five minutes, she was back in my room. She did not bother to knock again. I was pissed off.

"Do you fast?" she asked me.

"What?"

"Do you fast?"

"No, very rarely. Only when I feel like it."

Mansha stood resolute with her left hand on her left hip and her right hand up in the air.

"No, you must fast."

I replied bluntly, "*Didi*, I am not a religious person. I am spiritual to an extent. But I do what I want to do. To me, god is a very personal thing. I thank him in my own way."

"Good luck to you then because we are not such kind of people," said Mansha.

She was getting on my nerves now. Who the hell was she to give me instructions? I couldn't just change my personality for my in-laws. I wanted to shout at her and ask her to get out of my room but I didn't answer. Instead, I concentrated on organising my wardrobe. After a minute or two, Mansha left, thankfully shutting the door.

Tears rolled down my eyes. I was missing home and, on top of it, my sister-in-law was trying to intimidate me. I called mom.

"It's fine, *beta*. Ignore her. She will be leaving soon. It's your first day. So don't react. Please. Be good. Observe these people. You are new to them and so are they to you. Every family is different. You will get to know them slowly and you will handle them accordingly."

The mother's advice is so important for a daughter. I never bothered to call her when I was in college hostel. Now I was missing her badly. I felt as though I was among strangers.

My mother-in-law and Akansha were back. It was lunchtime. The food was ready. I started helping my mother-in-law set the table.

"You are not supposed to do any household work for a month at least," she said.

"Come on, mom. I can't sit idle for a month," I said.

"Let us serve you this time, Alisha. You can serve next time," said Mansha.

"I can ask serve you now too, *didi*."

Suddenly, Mansha looked at my forehead and asked, "Where is your *bindi*? You are married now. You have to wear a *bindi* along with the *sindoor*."

"I am wearing the *sindoor*."

"Yes, you are but you do not look as though you are married."

I was very irritated. Why was she after me? I burst out, "Then what proof does your brother carry or wear to show that he is married?"

There was silence for a minute. Then, after she found a reply, she said, "He wears a ring."

I smiled and said, "So do I."

Akansha chuckled. My mother-in-law was quiet. I should not have retorted I thought but Mansha was trying to intimidate me. I had to react. Wearing a sindoor or bindi is my choice as I am the one who who will wear them on my forehead,how could she command me on that?I wondered what my mother-in-law was thinking. Why didn't she say anything? This bothered me for some time. Then I just forgot about it.

6

Hitched

The best part of my relationship with Aryan was we never hesitated to speak our hearts out to each other. We discussed everything. I told him about Mansha. He asked me to ignore her as she would visit us only a few times in a year. She was his sister and she would remain so forever. So I didn't want to discuss this further.

I wondered if my mother-in-law was okay with what I did or said. Her silence didn't necessarily mean that she was okay with it. I guess I was thinking too much. I decided not to think over petty things.

Aryan and I went to Miami for our honeymoon. We had a fantastic time together. We were like college lovebirds again. I felt like a free bird with Aryan. I could do anything I wanted, without worrying about what others would think of me.

Aryan and I recollected the days when we were dating, before our wedding. We relived every moment.

I saw Aryan for the first time at the college dean's office. Or should I say I saw his back? We had been called to the office to fulfill some formalities. I stood behind Aryan waiting for my turn, while he was talking to someone. I felt a chill run down my spine. It was such a pure and pleasant feeling that I started blushing. I looked at his shoulders;

they were so broad with well-built muscles. He definitely was a gym person, I told myself. The perfume he was wearing made me hysterical. I felt like hugging him. While I was in my dream world, he left. I was upset, as I had not seen his face.

"Your documents, Miss Alisha," said the dean's assistant and I was back in reality. I wondered if he had seen me. Then I realised that I looked like a complete nerd, in my mom's loose *salwar* suit that nearly touched the floor. My hair was well- oiled and tightly plaited and I had bathroom slippers on. This was the attire the freshers had to come dressed in for a month, as part of ragging by the seniors. We juniors were their new toys.

The next day was the first day of our dentistry course. I waited for him and then he entered. I recognised him at first sight. He was tall, broad and handsome with a glowing face. I kept looking at his face, registering every feature. Then our eyes met for a second. I wanted these seconds to turn into minutes and hours. I felt my heart soaring.

I waited for days but he never approached me. Nor did I gather courage to go up to him and speak to him. Then, destiny played its part.

A month passed and our practical classes began. Aryan and I were in the same group. We talked for the first time.

"May I have your notes, please?" he asked me.

"Yes. Sure."

Then began our petty fights. He always borrowed my books and pens. I was irritated. This went on for over a month. We didn't exchange our phone numbers. Our conversations were restricted to the lab. Then came the college trip to Simla. More than half of our batch went on the four-day trip.

It was December. Snowfall welcomed us in Simla. The snow looked beautiful and pristine. We students decided to go on a walk through the streets. It was surreal. As we walked along the streets of Simla, Aryan joined me. We soon got talking. We talked about our likes, dislikes, hobbies and life in general. This was the real beginning of our friendship. We became very good friends. Then finally, the D-day arrived when he proposed his love for me. The proposal was simple and straightforward. Aryan confessed his feelings for me over the phone and asked me to be his girlfriend. I said 'yes'.

Years passed and we completed our graduation. There were only a few days before we would part ways. As the time to leave neared, my insecurity grew more and more. We both belonged to different states. Long distance relationships hardly work, I thought. Moreover, he had not asked me to marry him still.

Then came Valentine's Day. My girlfriends from college decided to throw a surprise party for their guys. Aryan was extremely happy. He loved the surprise. I told him to hold on to these memories as we didn't know what destiny had in store for us in the future. I was having my coffee when Aryan suddenly bent down on his knees. I had butterflies in my stomach. He extended his hand forward. He was holding a beautiful ring. He then popped the life-altering question, "Will you marry me?"

Without pausing to think, I said, "Yes, yes and yes."

The ring was there on my finger. We kissed and I was in seventh heaven.

We both were from different castes and cultures but thankfully, our parents were cool with it. Many love stories in college died a premature death because of differences in caste. I still remember the day when I told my mom about Aryan, she was so cool with it.

7

Back Home

Soon after the dreamy honeymoon, I was back to the real world where I was saddled with responsibilities. I was ready to do anything – cooking, cleaning and managing the house – because I loved Aryan a lot.

One morning, I was making French toast with Aryan in the kitchen.

"Have you given the souvenirs to everyone?" he asked

"Not yet. I will give them after breakfast."

"Okay, now listen to me. I want you to redecorate this apartment."

"What? Really?"

"Yes. Do whatever you want. It is your choice."

"Wow! Thank you, honey. I needed to hear that."

I planted a kiss on his forehead.

Everyone sat around the breakfast table chatting. Aryan and I were raving about the beauty of Miami to Akansha, my mother-in-law and my father-in-law. Suddenly Aryan said, "I want Alisha to redecorate this house."

My father in law said, "Yes why not? We would love for her to do that." My mother-in-law and Akansha were quiet. They had a vague smile on their faces.

"We will go shopping today afternoon," said Aryan.

"Good," said my father-in-law.

"Mom would you like to join us?" asked Aryan. "What will I do there? I guess Alisha's taste is different than mine."

Now I got it. My mother-in-law was hurt because I was going to redecorate the apartment she had put together. Being the oldest woman in the house, she did not want her authority to be undermined. She did not like me to take over. It was the classic case of hurt ego and insecurity. Akansha too was not ready to accept another woman in her life. I could sense this.

"So, what are you going to buy today? Have you made a list?" Akansha asked me.

"No, not yet. Aryan told me just today. I will make a list now," I said.

Soon Akansha left for work. She worked in a multinational company in Gurgaon.

"Alisha, I want to go to the grocery store nearby. You come with me," said my mother-in-law.

I accompanied her to the store. I discovered she was a miser. She bought only the things on her list. She didn't allow me to buy anything else. She simply said, "We don't need that now." Well, I do need it now, the voice in my head said. Suddenly, I felt the need to start working to be independent. Thank god Aryan was not a miser, I told myself.

Several thoughts clouded my head. My in-laws were so different from my parents. I was a part of this family now but I wondered how I could change myself. I could not change my personality just like that. I decided never to change but adapt instead.

We were back home. I went to my room to take some rest. I was in the middle of a nice nap when my phone rang. It was Aryan.

"Hey sweetheart. Get ready. I am coming to pick you up in 15 minutes."

I wore blue jeans and a long printed shirt. I went to my in-laws' apartment to inform my mother-in-law that I was going out. She scanned me from top to bottom but didn't say a word. I felt a bit uneasy. Then she said, "Okay. Bye." I rushed towards the lift.

Aryan and I went to a home décor store in a mall. We bought a sofa set, dining table and chairs, paintings, lamps and wall decals. The best part was Aryan didn't fuss about anything. I was happy.

When we got home, my mother-in-law came home and asked us what we bought. Aryan told her. Then came the question, "How much did you spend?"

"About 1.5 lakhs, mom," said Aryan.

"What? Oh my god! That is too much. You should not spend that much."

She shouted at the top of her voice.

"Mom! Please relax. These days, things are expensive. The things we have bought are worth the money."

"Maybe you guys know better. I am a fool."

She then left. Aryan got upset.

"Are you fine?" I asked.

"Yes. It is just that I want to live my life my way. I am a grown-up now. Mom should understand that."

Well, I wanted to tell him all this. But I tried to be nice and said, "Aryan, she is your mother. She won't advise you wrong."

"Yes, but I am not a kid anymore."

It was time for dinner. We all sat around the dinner table. I hoped there wouldn't be any more questions about our shopping.

"How was your day?"

"It was great, *papa*," I said.

"You guys have spent quite a lot of money. That's fine. I understand classy things are expensive these days." He winked at us before continuing. "Look Alisha, you are free to do anything. You are just like my daughter. I have given full freedom to Akansha. Yes, I was a bit strict with Mansha but one grows with time. I have learnt a lot, so will you. You are young right now. With time, you will learn how to manage everything in life. We are not the kind of people who bind their daughter-in-law. When I call you my daughter, I mean it. I am sure my wife Rita will not have any problem with your freedom."

"No, I don't have an issue. It's just that some things need to be done sensibly," my mother-in-law said.

"They are grown-ups, Rita. They will learn with time."

I was impressed. My father-in-law was very practical. He was the day's saving grace.

8

Girlfriends Meet

It was almost afternoon. Maria called me.

"Hello, girl! How are you doing? Hope I didn't disturb you. These days, you are not very active in the group. I got worried."

"Everything is fine, dear. It's just that I am busy in my new life."

"Busy… Hmm… Hope you guys are not making out the whole day."

"Shut up!"

"Okay, we girls have decided to catch up tomorrow at Cafe Coffee Day in Connaught Place and you are coming. At 4 p.m. No excuses."

"I will definitely come, silly. You don't worry."

"Okay. Then see you tomorrow."

"Yeah, we will have fun. See you."

"Who was it?" asked Aryan.

"That was Maria. All my girlfriends work in Delhi. We plan to meet tomorrow."

"That's good. You can take the car."

"Thanks."

I wore a long floral dress. I felt so fresh. I drove all the way alone in Delhi for the first time. I was irritated with the traffic. Finally, I reached my destination. I was late.

There were my girls. I felt so relieved seeing them. We hugged each other.

"You don't look like a newlywed Indian woman," said Ishika.

"Thank you! That is the complement I wanted."

"That is good. Your in-laws are relaxed."

"Well, I won't allow myself to be a showpiece to be paraded on the streets.

I saw that Nisha was quiet.

"How is your wedding shopping going on, Nisha?" I asked.

"I'm almost done with it. But I am in a fix over my wedding *lehenga*. I am torn between two outfits."

"How are you finding Delhi, my marriage guinea pig?" asked Maria.

"It's fine. Still adjusting."

I saw the look on Nisha's face. She seemed to be upset. I asked her, "Is everything fine, Nisha?"

Nisha looked at all three of us and said, "Yes. Actually, no."

"What happened?" we said together.

"My would-be sister-in-law is creating trouble between Anuj and me.

"What?" I asked.

"Yes. She makes up stories and tries to turn Anuj against me. She has already created a lot of misunderstanding between us. Anuj is not talking properly to me these days.

I don't know what to do. I can't tell him that his sister is a big liar. That will cause a huge problem."

"Do you mean to say instead of trusting you and listening to you, Anuj listens to his sister? You two have been engaged for more than six months. You said he really loves you. But honey, if he really loves you, why is he behaving like this? I think you deserve much better. Leave him," I told Nisha.

"What? What are you saying?"

"I am saying this because if this guy is choosing his family over you, this means you and Anuj do not share a strong bond."

"Oh stop it, Alisha," screamed Nisha.

"Calm down guys," said Ishika.

"Tell us everything, Nisha," said Maria.

"It was decided that Anuj's family would pay for the engagement function, out of the three wedding ceremonies. But now, as the wedding day is nearing, my sister-in-law has intervened. She is asking my family to spend on all three functions."

"And Anuj is not saying a word about this?" I asked.

"He says that if we wanted to get married, how does it matter who spends."

"How lame is that? Why is your sister-in-law doing all the talking? What about his parents?"

"They have given her all the responsibilities. She called up my mom and said that they could not spend any money and we had to fund all the ceremonies. My mom calmly told her that that was not possible. My sister-in-law was infuriated hearing my mother say 'no'. She twisted the whole conversation to Anuj. She said that my mother had been rude to her."

"What the hell! Look Nisha, we are your friends and we want to see you happy. I guess you are playing with fire here. If you jump into it, you will burn. It's not too late. Break up with Anuj. You deserve much better," said Maria.

"I can't. I love him. I have gone really far in this relationship."

I was agitated. "Goodness! Can't you see, woman? You love him but he and his family do not even respect you. You have gone blind."

Ishika intervened. "I think we should change the topic. Alisha, how is everything at your end? How is your new family?"

"They seem like nice people. I am still getting to know them. It's still early days. My father-in-law seems to be a practical man. Sister-in-law is mostly at work. The married one is a bit cranky. And my mother-in-law is a mystery."

Everyone laughed.

"How about Aryan?" Maria asked.

"He was a good boyfriend but he is an amazing husband."

We raised a toast with our coffee mugs.

9

Traditions Maintained

I was cooking in the kitchen when my mother-in-law came in and said, "Alisha, the *Navratra* festival is about to begin in a few days. I think we should start the preparations."

"Yes. Sure mom. But I don't know what is done during this festival."

"What? You don't know? You haven't observed any *Navratra* fast before?"

"No, mom."

"Didn't your mother fast?"

The conversation I had with Mansha flashed before my eyes. She was right in wishing me luck. I would need all the luck to get out of this tricky conversation, I thought to myself.

"No, mom."

"Really? That's surprising."

I didn't say anything.

"Okay, I will teach you how it is done. We will go out and buy clothes for the idols today. And I will decorate the prayer room at home."

"Oh, I would love to decorate too, mom."

"In our house, we have the practice of fasting for all nine days. We have only one meal in a day. Now quickly. Let's go."

I was stunned. I couldn't believe my ears. I shuddered at the thought of fasting for nine days. I could not do that.

"What happened? Are you okay?"

"Yes, mom. Don't you think nine days is a bit too much?"

"Oh, don't worry. I will accompany you. Aryan too will join you."

I smiled. "Really? Has Aryan fasted earlier?"

"No. It will be his first time too."

I was happy now. Aryan and I fasting together would be fun, I thought.

My mother-in-law and I went to the market to shop. I wanted to share my views on fasting with her. With great difficulty, I gathered courage. I opened my mouth and said, "Mom…"

"Yes."

"Is it necessary to fast? I mean, what if I don't?"

"No! You have to. It is our family tradition, culture and custom. This is our religion."

I did not prolong the conversation because I knew it would result in an argument.

We bought lights, clothes and some other things required for the *pooja*. I was happy. But I was also clueless as to how I would cope with the fast.

Back home, I decorated the prayer room. It was dinnertime when Aryan and my father-in-law came home. I showed them my work. They were happy.

"So, the *Navratras* are coming up?" asked my father-in-law.

"Yes, dad. Even I came to know about it today."

"Nice decoration," said Aryan.

"Yeah," said my father-in-law. "So, are you going to fast with us?"

I didn't reply. Aryan read my thoughts.

"How is the decoration I did?" asked my mother-in-law, as she entered the prayer room.

"You did it? But I thought that Alisha did it," said my father-in-law.

"It's one and the same thing," she said.

I didn't like what she said. I stared at her but she didn't look at me. I had done everything all alone, although my mother-in-law had promised to teach me how it was done. She was insecure about her place in the house. What else could it be, I thought.

After dinner, I locked the apartment door and went into our room. I saw Aryan lying on the bed and smiling at me.

"It's not funny," I said. "You know I am not that religious. I have my own way of offering my thanks to god. It is a personal and sensitive issue for me. I have my own bond and fasting is just not my thing."

"Relax, babe. We will find a way."

"What way? Even you have to fast with me."

"What? No."

"Don't worry, baby. We will find a way," I said, laughing.

"Wait, I have an idea."

"What?"

"Just pretend to mom that you are following everything she says. Do what she says. Pretend to fast. Whenever she is not around, eat what you want to. This way, she is also happy and you are also happy."

"Hmm... Not a bad idea. This way I will not offend her or hurt her feelings. Thanks for the idea. But what about you?"

"I will eat in office, obviously."

"We can have only one meal a day, according to your family tradition. That too in the evening."

Hmmm... This is not easy."

"I know..."

The fasting period began. We did *pooja* together. I was feeling very hungry. Time passed slowly. I saw the clock. It was just 10 a.m. I thought of having milk but I couldn't have even milk, according to the fasting rules. I thought of breaking the rules. After all, how would my mother-in-law know, I thought.

I went into the kitchen to have some snacks and milk. But something inside me stopped me. I thought why not give it a chance. I could try it. I knew it wouldn't be easy but I could try. So I continued to fast. I saw the clock. It was 12. I couldn't control my hunger. I rushed to the kitchen and ate a few biscuits. I broke my fast. This continued for all the nine days. Aryan and I ate in hiding like small children. I did feel bad for my mother-in-law. I asked god to forgive us. At least, my mother-in-law would not be hurt because she didn't know we had eaten on the sly.

Akansha was the only one who escaped the traditions of the house.

10

Space

One day, I was sitting on the sofa and watching TV when Akansha joined me.

"Nice song," she said.

"Yeah."

"You know *bhabhi*, I have got a project in Mumbai. I am moving there for a few months." "Wow! That's great. Congratulations."

"Thank you. Mom and dad are accompanying me to Mumbai. They will be there for a day or two. They want to see where I would be living and all that."

"Really? Mom didn't tell me this."

"I told them only today. I am leaving next Sunday. Thank god, I am leaving this place."

"Why so? Don't you like it here? Most of the times you are working or partying."

"I know but I want to stay alone. It will be just me in Mumbai and no one knows me there. It will be fun."

"Good, I like this positive side of yours. You are not afraid to explore."

"Yes *bhabhi*. I will go now and sleep in my room."

"Bye."

This was the first time Akansha and I had actually had a conversation. We hardly spoke to each other except to say 'hello' and 'bye'. Akansha was in a happy mood that day.

A week passed and Akansha left. Although we lived in two separate apartments, it always seemed one to me as every meal was cooked in my apartment and most of the time someone or the other was there. The idea of providing me with space after marriage was actually my false notion. Now that everyone was gone, I felt good. It would be only Aryan and I. I was so happy. I realised that Aryan and I would be having our own space after a long time. We could do anything. We could shout, dance, sing, make love anywhere, walk in shorts all around the house or walk naked and sleep naked. There was no need to worry about my mother-in-law ringing the doorbell. I decided to do something special that day. I went to the nearby market and bought several red roses and candles. I cooked my husband's favourite Chinese food. I lit up the entire apartment with candles and placed red roses at every corner. I wore a short black dress, which was Aryan's favourite. I was ready.

The doorbell rang. I opened the door. There stood Aryan, looking a bit surprised.

"Wow! You look lovely. Wait a minute," he said, looking at all the candles and the roses.

"You have done all this for me?"

"Yes, for you."

"That's so sweet. No one has ever done this for me."

"Hello! How could anyone else do all this for you when I am the only woman in your life?"

"Oh come here, my dear."

He pulled me towards him and we kissed. Aryan drew me to the floor and started undressing me. He kissed every part of my body and within minutes he was inside me. There were candles all around us and we were right in the middle. I was feeling on top of the world. I hadn't felt like this even during our honeymoon. We made endless love and Aryan was exhausted. It was time for another surprise. I brought out the champagne I had got for us and arranged the dinner table. Aryan was delighted to see all his favourite dishes.

"After so many days we are having 'we' time alone. I have been so caught up in routine that I have forgotten to do these small things for you. The small things that once made us happy… We don't get our private moments when the elders are around. We have also become like elders. I have decided that we will plan an outing every weekend to rekindle our love. After all, we are a newly married couple and I want us to remain like that always," said Aryan.

I kissed Aryan and said, "I hope so."

My in-laws were back a day later. I wished they had stayed for a week at least. I missed my 'day of freedom'. We were back to our routine. Then Sunday arrived. Aryan and I decided to go to the disco. I wore a nice little red dress. Aryan was getting ready.

"Gosh! You look so sexy," said Aryan.

"Thank you, dear," I said.

"But my mom is sitting in the living room."

"I wear western clothes at home too. She has never objected…"

"Yes. But you have never worn such as short dress in front of her. What if she objects to it?"

"Please, Aryan. We are going to a discotheque. I don't want to wear anything boring."

"Okay, do one thing. Wear leggings underneath and remove it in the car."

I looked at his face.

"What? Where do you get these ideas from?"

He chuckled.

I planted a kiss on his forehead and we went out.

"Mom, we are leaving," said Aryan.

"Oh. Okay. I will go to my apartment. Please come back on time."

"Yes, we will."

My mother-in-law stared at my outfit but she didn't say anything. She could have given a compliment I thought.

"Tomorrow we will all go out for dinner together. You should go out with your parents too, *beta*," said mother in law out of a sudden.

"Okay, mom. We are getting late. Bye."

I was annoyed. "I think your mom feels insecure."

"What? Where did this come from?"

"Didn't you hear what did she just say?"

"Oh, come on. You are taking it all wrong. She wants to go out with us. It has been a long time. That is it."

"Yeah. Maybe I am wrong."

"Let's party!"

We hit the floor like two crazy people and had a gala time.

The next evening, my mother-in-law was ready to go out for dinner. She was ready much before time. She wore a beautiful cream *sari* with a pearl necklace. She looked graceful. I too decided to wear something ethnic. I chose a nice party suit. We were ready. Looking at us, Aryan started laughing. "Mom and Alisha, we are going out for dinner, not to someone's wedding."

"Oh! Please *beta.* I hardly get a chance to get dressed like this," said my mother-in-law.

"Okay then, let's go."

We picked up my father-in law-from his office and went to a boring fine-dine restaurant. Classical music was being played.

"Wow, nice music," said my father-in-law.

"Hmm…" That was as what I managed to say.

"Let us order some Indian food today," said my father-in-law.

"That we can eat at home too, dad," said Aryan.

"Yes, but home food is not like restaurant food. You know old people's stomach cannot digest any other kind of food."

We gave up and ordered *dal, roti* and *sabzi.* I was indeed bored.

We went out for dinner as a family three times that month and then Aryan and I were done. These outings were stifling. We had to get out of it smartly. We decided to go out just twice in a month – one outing with my in-laws and the other just the two of us though we managed to sneak out quite many times all alone.

11

The Secret

I was done decorating my house. It took me three months to organise it. I also gradually learnt to cook. Cooking was no more a hassle for me. In fact, I enjoyed it.

One evening, I decided to make something special. I invited Aryan's uncle, Vimal and his family, for dinner. He was my father-in-law's real brother. Vimal uncle and his wife were both surgeons. They had two daughters. The older one was married and settled abroad and the younger one Mira was in college, pursuing her masters in physics. I was impressed. They were very intelligent people. I was meeting them for the first time after the wedding.

"Wow! *Bhabhi,* the house looks beautiful. You have given a complete facelift to the house," said Mira.

"Thank you," I said.

"Yes, *beta.* It's beautiful. Good work," said Vimal uncle.

"Thank you again."

I was delighted.

"You have got a really talented daughter-in-law," said my aunt to my mother-in-law.

My mother-in-law paused for a few seconds and then said, "Hmm..."

I really wished she would appreciate my hard work and praise me for it. I was not able to figure out her character. On the second day after my wedding, she had supported me in front of her daughter. Now she was showing traits of insecurity. Someday I wanted to tell her that I was her son's wife and she had to accept that reality.

The women sat in the lobby, while the men used the balcony for drinks and snacks. I had made fish fry, bread rolls, *dhokla* and vegetable nuggets.

"*Bhabhi*, you are really a good cook," said Mira.

"Oh! You like them? Thank you so much."

"Who taught you cooking?" asked aunty.

"Google."

"You are really a smart girl."

My mother-in-law could not tolerate these compliments. So she excused herself and went into the kitchen to bring some snacks. I was really enjoying the company of uncle, aunty and Mira. I was having fun. After all, there was someone to appreciate me. I wished my sister-in-law too had been here. It would have been a good opportunity to bond with her.

"When are you starting your dental practice?" asked aunty.

Before I could reply, my mother-in-law intervened and said, "I think it's too early now. She should first adjust to the new family."

I was appalled at what she said.

"But Rita, don't forget that she is a professional too. Don't make her a homemaker if she wants to work," said aunty.

Aunty was my saviour for the day.

"Yes, she can work if she wants. It's up to her."

'Sure I want to. I want to enjoy and settle down in this city. Once, I am comfortable, I will open my own clinic,' I told myself.

I went to the balcony to offer some snacks to the men. The three men were enjoying their drinks and discussing fish.

I could see that Aryan was enjoying the company of his father and uncle.

"Very interesting topic for discussion," I said.

"Ha ha! Thank you! By the way, everything is delicious," said Vimal uncle.

"Thank you, uncle. But please have some space in your stomach. These are just the starters."

It was past 10 p.m. We decided to set the table for dinner. It was getting late. But before setting the table, I wanted to go to the washroom. I went to the guest room to use the washroom there. But before I could open the door, I heard a noise from inside. Someone was speaking inside the washroom. I was about to leave but then I heard something I should not have heard.

"Baby! Don't be angry. I was busy at work today. Tomorrow, I will definitely meet you. You are my *jaan.* I love you and you know that."

I could not believe my ears. I felt as though the whole world around me was spinning. My father-in-law was having an affair.

12

The Dilemma

I was not able to sleep the whole night. One part of me wanted to tell everything to Aryan and the other part was saying a big NO. We both shared almost everything with each other but this was something related to his father. Not just something but a huge thing. I could not find the courage to tell him. What if I was wrong? This was something I could not share even with my girlfriends. Only one person came to my mind. My mother.

The next morning, after everyone was done with breakfast, I called mom.

"Hi dear, how are you?"

"Not at all well, mom"

"Why? What happened?"

"There is something really important I want to tell you mom. I think my father-in-law is having an affair."

"What? Really?"

"Yes. I heard him talking to someone on the phone yesterday. He was addressing someone 'baby'. Now I get it. This is why he comes home late these days. In fact, on some days he doesn't come home at all. He says he has some important work to do and has to stay back in office. He then comes only the next day."

"And he does some other work. Hmm… Does Aryan know this?"

"No, he does not. I don't think so."

"Okay. Don't tell him anything. This is a very sensitive issue. It could break your home in seconds. Your happy family will no more be happy. Don't take any step for now. Let things be the way they are. You spill the beans only when you have proof. You need to have proof, otherwise these people may misunderstand you. Look, you have just got married. Don't take any rash step."

"Okay, mom. You are right"

My mom was right, I thought. She always was my saviour. I didn't know how I would survive without her. I wouldn't tell anyone anything. Let the time be right, I told myself.

13

Freedom as it is

As time passed, I forgot the incident. I wasn't even sure if I was right but a troubling thought always lingered in my heart. I decided not to think about it and ignore it.

I wanted to go to the spa. It had been a long time since I had pampered myself. I decided to drive the car myself. I was driving after a long time. I was so tensed that I violated many traffic rules. Driving in the big city was a huge challenge for me. It would take some time for me to adapt to the traffic in Delhi. Finally, I found a nice spa. After looking around for a long time, I found space to park. As I stepped out of the car, the scorching sun burnt my face in seconds. I had to adapt to the Delhi heat too. Not to mention, the crowd. Well, this is the life I wanted, I thought to myself. I was missing my beautiful Manali.

My hometown was very beautiful with lovely landscapes. It was a small town in which every third person knew who I was. There was no noise pollution. It was just you and nature.

I was getting a bit bored in Delhi. Many of my schoolmates had settled in Delhi but they were all busy. They had only time for their family, after working hard through the week.

Passing time was the biggest challenge in a big place like Delhi. Every place seemed so far, thanks to the traffic snarls.

I went inside the spa and relaxed. I felt so relieved. After an hour of getting pampered, I didn't feel like going home as yet. I went to a coffee shop. I felt good doing all this alone. It was just me and no one else around.

Sometimes spending time alone can do a lot of good. I hadn't done this after marriage. I felt like a free bird.

As I was having my coffee, I saw two women sitting around the table next to mine.

"I am fed up of my mother-in-law. If I have to go out, I have to take her permission. Am I a kid who would get lost? I have to take her permission to meet my parents or stay with them. Do you know what happened last time I went to my parents' place? I had taken her permission to stay for a week but she called me home in just two days."

"Why?" the other woman said.

"Because my mother-in-law had to buy bedsheets and wanted me to go with her."

"What? Seriously? Ha ha…"

I wanted to laugh, but I controlled my laughter. I just chuckled.

"Yes, she does this intentionally. She doesn't want me to be me. I quit my job for these people. What else do they want? Their first condition was that I quit my job. Because of my age and pressure from my parents, I said 'yes'. The guy is nice but it's an arranged marriage. We are still getting to know each other. We have not yet reached a stage where I can share my feelings with him. I am afraid of something going wrong. I am stuck. I have so much mental stress."

"Talk to your parents about it then."

"I have. They say I have to adjust."

I had heard enough and I couldn't stop myself from intervening.

"Excuse me, would you mind if I told you something?"

"What?" asked the woman with the problem with her in-laws.

"I am sorry that I heard your conversation. I just want to say please don't let anyone over-rule you. Be bold enough from the beginning. I am not asking you to fight. Speak your heart out, patiently. Things may then change."

"Thanks for your advice, but it's my personal matter."

"I am sorry."

Stupid me. Why did I have to butt in like that with this feminist streak of mine? I headed to the parking lot and thanked my stars that I did not have an overbearing mother-in-law. She gave me my space. But I still had issues with her. I felt stupid.

I reached home and made my mother-in-law tea and *pakoras* with love.

"You have never made *pakoras* till now. Anything special today?" she asked.

"Nothing. I just felt like making them." She smiled and said, "Thank you."

She was not that bad I thought. She never objected to my clothes or anything I did. At least I had my identity.

14

Nisha's Wedding

Finally, it was Nisha's turn to get married. Personally, I didn't want this to happen. In fact, none of us wanted her to get into this marriage. But love is blind. So blind that one cannot even make out what's wrong. Nisha had this notion that everything would be fine after the wedding but I was doubtful. If all is not well before the wedding, then how can you expect things to change miraculously afterwards? I prayed for her to be happy forever and hoped everything would turn out fine.

Aryan and I entered the wedding venue. It was beautifully decorated in gold, red and white flowers and yellow lights. We went to the bridal room and there she was. A beautiful bride in a red *lehenga* looking gorgeous like never before. What was adding to her beauty was the happiness on her face. She was excited.

"I wish you remain happy forever," I told Nisha.

"Thank you, my dear," said Nisha.

Then came Ishika dressed in a royal blue suit. She was looking fabulous.

"Hello, my pretty girls," she said posing. I understood what she wanted and said, "Okay, you are looking fabulous."

"Thank you," she said laughing.

We started clicking pictures. I could see Aryan was getting bored. I excused myself and went out with Aryan to eat something. While we were eating, Maria came with her boyfriend Raj.

Raj was the marketing head of a big advertising firm in Noida. He was about six feet tall, fair, and very handsome. He was a Delhiite and Maria was a girl from the mountains. Maria's parents were from Kerala, but her parents had shifted to Manali before she was born. She was a dusky beauty with killer looks. She was five feet seven inches tall. They were contrasting in complexion but they looked great together. Maria introduced us to Raj, who was her boss. We chatted for a while. Then we girls excused ourselves.

"I think he is about to propose to me," said Maria.

"Wow! Best of luck, girl," I said.

"Cool, so you too are going to become a martyr soon," said Ishika.

Maria looked at me and asked, "You tell us, how is everything going on?"

"It's going great. I am planning to open my clinic soon. I can't sit at home anymore. I have to start my practice."

"Have you talked to Aryan about it?" asked Ishika.

"No, what is the need? I am sure he won't have any issue. After all, he too is a dentist. Never mind the fact that he left it and joined his father in business."

The *baraat* arrived. We went downstairs. The sound of the firecrackers and the lights from the fireworks made the place ethereal. It reminded me of my wedding day. We girls dream about this day for long. When the time actually comes, everything is over in a flash. But the memories remain with us forever.

Anuj was looking handsome but I was more interested in seeing Nisha's sister-in-law. She seemed to be happy. This made me think positively. I again prayed for Nisha's happiness. There was happiness all around. Aryan and I wished Nisha good luck and left.

15

Misunderstood

On our way back home, I told Aryan that I wanted to start my practice.

"What? Why do you want you work? We are doing well financially."

I was stunned at his reaction.

"Are you serious? I never said we are not well financially and that's why I wanted to work."

Aryan had a confused look on his face.

"Baby, you are getting me wrong. I didn't mean that. I want you to relax, sit at home, and pamper yourself. I don't want you to take on any stress. We have everything you want."

"Gosh Aryan! I did not expect this from you. I am not the kind of woman who wants to sit at home and relax. And you are talking about stress! I feel stressed at home. I have given my five years to be what I am today. I have to practice my profession. Only that will help me relax and make me happy. I can't waste my education. You switched to your father's business because you wanted to. It was your choice and I respect that. I want to work, for dentistry is my passion. I want to earn my own money rather than depend on you."

"Okay,calm down, you want this. It will happen then."

"That is not only the reason. When I start working, I will come in contact with the outside world. I will become more confident. I feel like I am losing it all sitting at home."

"Hmm… Okay sweetheart, go ahead. I am with you."

The next morning, after everyone was done with their breakfast, I decided to do some research on dental clinic interiors on my laptop. As I was browsing the internet, my mother-in-law came in and sat next to me. She peered into my laptop screen and asked me, "What are you searching for?"

As though she did not know, I thought to myself. After all, she had read what was on the screen.

"I have decided to open a dental clinic. I think I should start my practice."

"Why? Are you not happy at home?"

"Mom, that's a weird question. Of course, I am happy at home. But I will be happier if I start working."

"How will you manage home then?"

"I don't know. But I will. You will be there at home, *na*?"

"Hmm… Yes, I can manage my apartment. It won't be easy for an old lady to manage two houses."

That's odd, I thought. Since the day I got married, I had been managing everything in both the apartments – from cooking to supervising the maid. But when I needed her support, my mother-in-law was not ready to help. Shouldn't she be happy that she would get her power and authority back, I wondered.

"Mom, leave it to me. I will manage."

"Alisha, you have got everything. We have all the money. Why do you want to work?"

"Because your son has married a professional. He is a professional too. I will have my own clinic. It's like a dream come true for me."

"So, you have talked to Aryan."

"Yes."

That was it. She didn't say anything. When she knew that I had Aryan's support, she backed off. But I still couldn't understand why she wouldn't want me to work. Didn't she get it that it was not about the money but about passion and dreams?

16

Trouble

A week passed by. I started planning the interiors of my clinic, the marketing strategy, and the logistics. I was making a list of things to do when my phone rang. It was Nisha's mom. I was surprised.

"Hello, *beta*. I am sorry to bother you."

"No aunty. It's absolutely fine. You sound anxious. What's the matter?"

"Did you speak to Nisha recently?"

"No aunty. I just texted her asking how everything was. She replied that she was busy and that I should give her some time to settle down in the new environment."

"We did a big mistake."

I could hear her sobbing.

"Please tell me, aunty. Is everything fine?"

"I called Nisha yesterday. She was upset. She was obviously crying but she didn't tell me much except that she hoped everything would turn out well with time. She also said that she couldn't talk to me and would call me later."

"Give me some time, aunty. I will find out what is going on. You don't worry. Nisha is a brave girl."

What was happening to Nisha? I was worried. She should have told her mom everything. I called my girlfriends and told them what was happening. None of us had spoken to her. I decided to call her. I called but there was no response. Then I texted her. After half an hour, Nisha replied: 'Hi dear. I am doing well. Will call you after some time.'

I waited for her call. After a few minutes, my phone rang.

"Hello," I said. I could hear her sobbing.

"What's the matter, dear? Please tell me."

"You girls were right. I should have listened to you. Nothing has changed even after the wedding. My sister-in-law is still a troublemaker. The morning after our wedding day, she entered my room and asked me to show the clothes I had bought. She shouted at me. She criticised my taste and choice. She took out all my lingerie and threw them on the bed and accused me for being obscene. My mother-in-law didn't say anything but she didn't stop my sister-in-law too. My sister-in-law told me that I must not wear 'obscene' clothes. Don't I have the right to wear what I want in front of my husband?"

I was agitated and said, "How dare she say that? She has some mental disorder, I am telling you. How can she take away your freedom?"

"Not only this. She said the whole wedding arrangement was not up to the mark. It was not worthy of their status."

"They have no status, believe me. They can never be happy. Your wedding was fabulous."

"They woke me up at 4 in the morning and asked me to do all the household work, including cooking. They knew even before the wedding that I didn't know how to cook.

They earlier said they had no issues with that. Yes, I learnt the basics before the wedding but my sister-in-law asked me to make the toughest of dishes. Anuj saw all this but he never said a word. He was the one who didn't let me buy ethnic clothes because he liked me in western clothes. He said since we would be living in Malaysia, I should buy more western clothes. But he has totally changed now. Since our wedding day, we haven't gone out at all. No lunch or dinner, no honeymoon too. We are not like a newly married couple."

(Anuj was working in Malaysia on a project for an advertising company.)

Tears rolled down my eyes. I composed myself and said, "Don't worry. You guys will be leaving in a week. Things will get better when you both are alone."

"No, you have no idea what these people are up to. They have already started plotting. They do not want Anuj to take me along. They want me to serve them here. My sister-in-law is married but 12 out of 24 hours, she is at my home."

"What? That's weird."

"Anuj wants to take me with him, thankfully. I will find a way."

"Look, if no one supports you, you have to stand up for yourself. I am really surprised that you, a well-educated and independent girl, who has worked and lived in a city like Delhi all alone, is tolerating all this. Seriously, what has happened to you? Why aren't you fighting back? By being submissive, you are giving them the power to intimidate you more and more."

"I don't want them to think that I am rude. That is why I do not retort."

"That's so silly of you, Nisha. What about them torturing you?"

"I am putting up with all this for Anuj. I love him. I know he will change."

Love is seriously blind, I thought.

"Whatever. Call your mom and please speak your heart out to her. She is really worried."

"Okay, I will."

17

Surprise Visits

Nisha finally went to Malaysia along with her husband. Though I didn't speak to her before she left, I was happy that finally she got some space.

I was inaugurating my clinic. All relatives and friends in Delhi were invited. I was dressed in a south Indian green silk *sari*. I wore a *gajra* on my hair. I was very happy. I thanked Aryan for helping me at every step. Without his support, I could not have made it. Everyone around me was happy except my mother-in-law. And Akansha didn't care. I had learnt to ignore them. I tried to be me and if they did not like it, it was their problem. At least, they never played politics in the house and they let Aryan and me be the way we were. I was thankful to them for that.

The head of the municipal corporation was the chief guest. The ribbon was ready to be cut when I saw a young lady join us. She was really beautiful. Then I saw my father-in-law and husband greeting her. I was so busy observing them that I didn't even notice that the ribbon was already cut. The sound of people clapping brought me back from my reverie.

My father-in-law introduced me to her.

"Alisha, meet Neha. She is our new secretary. She just joined office yesterday."

"Hello," she said, "Nice to meet you, ma'am. Many congratulations on your big day."

"Thank you so much. And nice to meet you too. Please make yourself comfortable. Have some drinks and snacks," I said and excused myself.

I pulled Aryan towards me and asked, "Who is she?"

"You met her, right?"

I rolled my eyes. "I must tell you that your new secretary has no dressing sense at all. I mean, she is wearing a red-hot club dress for a clinic inauguration. Who does that? And why do you hire such a young lady as secretary?"

Aryan burst out laughing. "You are so jealous. Take a chill pill, my dear. I am not interested in her. I have eyes only for you. I have a hotter woman to hit on."

"Oh, shut up!"

"The old secretary left. So we hired her. She is smart and educated."

"Hmmm… Whatever it is, I am really getting insecure. You should not be surrounded by such young, smart and beautiful women. I will keep an eye on her."

I winked.

"Where are your girlfriends, Alisha?" asked my mother-in-law.

"They will be here soon."

Finally, they made it. I was so happy to see my girls. Only Nisha was missing.

"That is one hot chick," exclaimed Maria, looking at Neha.

"Yeah," said Ishika.

"She is Neha. New secretary for the office. Okay, leave her now. Tell me, what's going on?"

"First take us around your clinic, girl."

I showed the girls the clinic. They really loved the interiors. I was delighted.

Then I took the girls home for lunch.

But Ishika got a call from her boss and she left. It was just Maria and me.

"How is Raj?"

"He is fine."

"So, when are you guys getting married?"

"I don't know. There are many hurdles."

"What hurdles?"

"I wanted to tell you before. Let me tell you now. His family is not ready to accept me as their daughter-in-law. They don't have any issue with my religion but surprisingly my skin colour is the problem. They want a fair daughter-in-law who is 'presentable' to their people."

"Don't tell me that. These people are trying to undermine your confidence. What does Raj say?"

"Thankfully, he supports me. He says he would never leave me. He tries to boost my ego all the time by saying I am beautiful. He says we will wait for a few months and if his family does not support us, we will get married without them."

"Great! He is ready to leave his family for you. I am impressed. What else do you want?"

"I want his family to accept me happily."

"But if they don't, they are not worth it. They have small minds. You cannot make their minds grow big in a day. The best part is Raj is with you."

Finally the day was over. Maria left. I wished that things really turn out well at her side. Raj belonged to a very well educated and high class family. I was really astonished to hear all this from Maria.

18

Caught in a Double Drama

It was my first day at work. It was a good start. I had already seen a patient. It was past twelve and I was checking the messages on my phone. There were so my congratulatory messages from all and sundry, except Nisha. It had been a week since she left. Her phone was switched off. Memories of the wonderful times we girls had flashed in my mind. We were friends for life but marriage was slowing things a bit.

I called Maria and Ishika on a phone conference.

"Hello girls," I said.

"I was about to call you," said Maria

Ishika said, "Nisha's mom called me. She said Nisha's phone has been switched off since the day she left India. Neither Nisha nor her husband has called her. Nisha's parents do not understand what is going on. They do not know anyone in Malaysia."

"This is getting really serious. I am going to punch that Anuj on his face," said Ishika.

"Chill, Ishika. We don't know has happened or is happening. But whatever it is, I hope everything is fine. I have an idea. Maybe Anuj will answer our call. I will call him. I have his number," I said.

"Yes. Not a bad idea," said Maria.

I called Anuj. As the phone rang, my heart beat grew faster…

Finally, Anuj answered his phone. "Hello, who's this?"

"HI…this is Alisha, Nisha's friend."

"Oh hi! How are you, Alisha?"

His voice was charming.

"I was trying to call Nisha but her phone is switched off. I have left her a message on Facebook."

"Aaaa… She's fine. I will do one thing. Right now, I am in office. When I reach home, I will tell her to call you."

"Okay, fine. I will wait for her call."

At 6:30 p.m., my phone rang. It was from a new number.

I answered, "Hello."

"Hi Alisha. Nisha here. I am fine. Look, my phone is on loudspeaker. Anuj is here with me. Anything important?"

"No. I just wanted to know how you are."

"I will get a new number in a few days. I will call you then, okay?"

She then hung up.

There was something fishy going on. Why was the phone on loudspeaker?

I made a conference call. Nisha's mom was also present. I told her everything and asked her if she knew anything. She told us that Nisha's in-laws had criticised everything they had bought. "They didn't appreciate any of the outfits we bought for Nisha. They didn't like the clothes we had given them too. So I told them that I would buy a new set of clothes if they didn't like them. I said so, hoping they wouldn't bother my girl. They instead got offended and made an issue out of it. Since then, Aryan has not been talking to me. He is also not allowing my girl to talk to us."

"Issues can be made out of anything. I don't know what has happened to Nisha. Even she is acting weird," said Ishika.

"She is just following her husband's instructions because she wants to save this marriage," said Nisha's mom.

"She will call you soon, aunty. You need not worry. I spoke to her and she seemed okay," I said.

I was agitated. I drank gallons of water and calmed myself.

"Honey, shall we go home?" Aryan asked me. I hadn't even noticed that Aryan was in my clinic.

I looked at my watch. It was 8 p.m.

"I will come soon. You go. I just want to finish something."

"Are you sure?"

"Yes dear."

Aryan left.

After 15 minutes, Aryan called me and said, "Alisha, I forgot my other cellphone in office. Can you go to my office on your way home and get it?"

"But office will be closed now."

"No, dad is there. He is staying in office today. He has some important work to do."

"Okay, I will get it."

Aryan's office was in the building just one block away from my clinic. I was about to enter the office when I heard some noise. It was of giggling and laughing. I opened the door with a big shove and saw what I wished I had not seen. Neha was sitting on my father-in-law's lap and tickling him.

I was shocked and said, "Dad…"

"Alisha…"

I quickly turned and ran towards my car and left for home. I was trembling. I calmed myself, took a deep breath, and drove home. I was home in five minutes. I pressed the doorbell as hard as possible.

"Relax, I am opening the door," Aryan said.

I was trembling.

"What's wrong?" he asked. "Gosh, why are you trembling? What's the matter? Please tell me."

"Your father… Your father is having an affair with Neha," I said, stuttering.

"What? What are you saying?"

"I am saying what I saw. She was sitting on his lap and cuddling him as I entered the office. Remember that day when we had invited Vimal uncle and his family for dinner, he was in the washroom and I heard him addressing someone 'baby'."

"Why didn't you tell me then?"

"Because I was not very sure. I mean, he is your father. I didn't have any proof and I thought what if I had heard it wrong."

Aryan rushed to the other apartment and shouted, "Mom, please come out. We need to go."

"What is the matter with you? Why are you shouting?"

"I will tell you everything. Just come with me."

My heart was thumping. Aryan left to the office with his mom. Thank god Akansha was not there. She had gone to Bangalore on some other project, after her Mumbai stint. I was getting restless; I took my car and headed to the office. It took some courage for me to enter the office. I saw that Neha had vanished.

"There she is," said my father-in-law. "How can you accuse me of indecency? I have always treated you like my daughter. I never expected this out of you."

I was astonished. He was the man I admired the most in this house. I couln't believe my ears. Everyone looked at me as if I was the culprit. The tables had turned. I wanted to shout at him but instead tears rolled down my eyes.

"Why are you doing this, dad?"I said…my throat choking.

"Now, you don't act so innocent. I know you want to break up the house and live alone with Aryan. That is why you set this up," said my mother-in-law.

"She didn't set this up, mom. I had left my cellphone in office and I asked her to get it," Aryan finally spoke up.

"Oh, come on *beta*. Can't you see that she wants to break this house? She is such a spendthrift. She wants to take all our money and property and separate you from us. See, it has already been a year since you got married. She hasn't even planned a kid."

"What? Have you gone crazy, mom? It is our mutual decision not to have a kid now. Don't you dare say anything against her. I didn't know your heart was so filled with poison. You believe what you want to believe. I trust her. She is my wife, don't forget that. And dad, I don't want to see that secretary tomorrow. From now on, both of you stay away from Alisha. I will sell our apartment soon and move to a new one. And dad, it would be better if we restrict our talks to business only. I will soon leave and start a new company."

"No *beta*, please don't leave us alone," said my father-in-law.

Aryan pulled my arm and dragged me out of the office. As I entered my room in the apartment, Aryan hugged me tight and said, "The world may turn against you but I never will. I trust you and I believe you. I will always stand by you. I am sorry for what my family said. I know my dad is lying. I was suspicious about their relationship."

"My intension was never to break this family," I said weeping.

"No need to say anything. You didn't break it. They did."

19

The Change

Everything changed. There was no more casual talking, no more eating together, and no get-togethers. I was depressed. I had given my hundred per cent to this family, embraced it as my own family, and in turn I was disowned. I had done things I had never done before for the family. I had turned from a lazy woman to an enterprising daughter-in-law. I had cooked for them, decorated the house, greeted them and their guests, and even cancelled my outings to finish the household chores but everything was in vain.

I was shattered. I was not at fault but I felt guilty. Aryan loved his parents and he was more hurt than I was. I wondered what would have happened if he hadn't stood by me. That would have been the end of our marriage. I thanked god for blessing me with a husband like Aryan. Our relationship was like lemon and soda – sparkling and frothy. We displayed extreme emotions. We fought hard but made up quickly too, as though nothing had happened. Some women had told me that their boyfriends had changed after marriage. Yes, Aryan too had changed but for the better.

I called my mom and told her everything. She was so angry and wanted to come and intervene with my father in law. I begged her to calm down and not interfere. I also asked her not to disclose anything to dad. He would get really upset and this could trouble his health. I knew that I was his weakness. That would only make things worse. She agreed with me that was the mature thing to do and stayed away.

Days passed. My in-laws and I were still not on speaking terms. Then one day, I came home from the clinic for lunch. The doorbell rang. I was surprised to see my mother-in-law standing outside. After all that had happened, I was in no mood to welcome her inside. I said in a firm voice, "Yes."

"Please, may I come in?"

"Aryan asked me to stay away from you."

"Please."

I could no longer be hard on her, so I let her in. We sat on the sofa. Then she said, "I am sorry."

I couldn't believe my ears.

"I am sorry about what I said. I was so wrong. I know I have hurt you a lot. Please, please forgive me. I believed my husband blindly that I didn't think I could be wrong. I checked his cellphone yesterday and read his old chat transcripts with that secretary. I was shattered. I didn't question him. If I question him, we will end up divorced. He will never admit the truth. It has been 28 years. I thought I should give him another chance as I didn't find any chat scripts after the incident. Maybe your father in law is trying to change. I can't leave this family. Aryan and my daughters are my world. Where will I go leaving them? I am not even that educated," saying this

she broke down.

I didn't know what to do. How could a woman put up with all this? Her husband didn't love her and she didn't even bother to question him because she feared it would all end.

"What's wrong with you, mom? If he is wrong, you should confront him. We are with you. We will support you."

"If I do confront him, this family will be destroyed. And what will my daughters think?"

"If I were in your place, I would fight."

"But I am not you. I don't have a husband like Aryan. You please don't tell anything to Aryan or anyone else about this. I want my son back. Only you can make him understand that I am sorry for what has happened. I inflicted my insecurities on you and I am really sorry for that. I hope you will forgive me."

That is a big thing for a mother in law to accept that she's insecure of her daughter in law. I bent down on my knees and held her hand and said, "It is fine, mom. I will talk to Aryan. You don't worry."

I felt I should forgive her. After all, she had opened her heart to me. She had forgiven her husband who had cheated on her. That needed lots of courage and a generous heart. It is not an easy thing to do. My forgiveness was nothing in front of hers. I would not have had the heart to forgive my husband had I been in her place. My mother-in-law was a woman,if not strong but a big heart. But I think she had no other choice either…as she said.

20

Welcome Mansha

Things were slowly getting back to normal. Aryan began talking to his parents. He forgave his dad too, eventually. But I never talked to his dad. I maintained my distance. We pretended that everything was normal in front of other people. Maybe with time, I would forgive him too.

The addition to my daily routine was an early morning walk with my mother-in-law. Aryan was surprised when he came to know this. "I wish things remain well between you two forever," he said, winking. I smiled. My mother-in-law and I enjoyed our walks together. We talked about nature, the weather, relatives, food and just about anything under the morning sky.

One morning, my mother-in-law told me that Mansha was coming along with her kids for a few days. "All the best to me," I muttered under my breath.

The day when Mansha was about to arrive, I made an elaborate lunch before leaving to the clinic. When I returned home in the afternoon, I saw that my flat was open. Mansha had occupied a room in my apartment instead of staying with her parents.

"I thought I will get a chance to know you more if I stayed here," said Mansha. What surprised me was that she didn't even say 'hello' to me after I welcomed her and gave her a hug.

"Did you have your lunch?" I asked.

"No, not yet."

"Okay, I will set the table for you then."

"No, I am not hungry right now. My kids have had their lunch and so has mom. She has gone to take a nap. You eat."

"Okay, fine." I didn't insist on Mansha eating along with me.

Aryan and I got back home late at night. Mansha and her boys were done with dinner. Aryan greeted and hugged his sister and nephews and went inside our room to change. I set the dinner table. My mother-in-law and father-in-law had also finished dinner and had gone to their apartment. Aryan and I were about to eat when Mansha said, "Aryan, you have changed after marriage."

Aryan's reply was classic. "Yes, just like your husband changed after he married you."

We burst out laughing. Masha was irritated.

Aryan chatted with Mansha for some time. Then we went into our room. It was about 12:30 p.m. Aryan and I were watching a movie when suddenly someone started banging our door.

"Aryan, Aryan…"

It was Mansha.

Aryan immediately went outside.

"What's the matter?"

"I want to talk to my husband. He hasn't called me."

"Then call him."

"My phone balance is over. It's prepaid."

Aryan gave her his phone. When she was done talking, Mansha gave him back the phone.

Aryan saw the look on my face and said, "Sorry, it won't happen again."

The next day, I took out the buns I had bought the previous day and made *aloo tiki* burgers for breakfast for the kids. Just then, Mansha came in and said, "My kids don't eat junk."

"You should have told me that while I was making them. I thought they would like it."

"Do you have Maggi?"

"Yes, it's on that shelf, you can make it."

I told her to make it herself before she had the chance to ask me.

Even Maggi is junk, I thought. I didn't know what was she up to.

It was 11:30 p.m. We were really tired and were about to sleep when someone banged our door again. It was Mansha, of course.

"What is it?" Aryan went outside and asked her.

"I can't find green tea."

"You want to have green tea at this time? You banged our door for green tea? Have you gone crazy?"

He gave her the tea and came back.

"Sorry, it won't happen again," he said.

Night three:

It was midnight. Everyone was asleep. Aryan and I were making out when we heard our door banging again.

"Aryan... Aryan..."

Aryan rushed to the washroom. Mansha had banged the door so hard that the lock gave away. I was lying on my bed in my lingerie. Well, she needed to see this. I covered myself with the bedsheet and said, “Do you know what time it is? How can you bang someone’s door like this? We need some privacy here, please.”

“So… So sorry,” Mansha said. She was embarrassed and left.

I got up and bolted the door.

Aryan came out of the washroom and asked, “What was that?”

“Now, it won’t happen again,” I said.

21

Courage to Bear

Mansha left the day after. She was so embarrassed that she hardly made any eye contact before she left. She had learnt a lesson. What a relief that was. My house resembled a playground with things strewn all around. I cleared the mess.

It was my off day. So I made a video call to Nisha and was shocked to see that she had become really thin.

"What has happened to you? You have gone so thin."

"I have lost 15 kilos," said Nisha.

"Are you okay? Is Anuj treating you well? It's been a long time since we talked."

"Our relationship is slowly improving. But we will be coming back to India soon. The company has let go of a few people."

"Oh no!"

"I will be back to the hell hole. Even here, when my sister-in-law calls Anuj, his behaviour towards me changes."

"Look Nisha. Please don't stay quiet. Speak up if she tortures you. Look at you, stress has eaten you up."

"You know the day when you called and I had put my phone on speaker, Aryan took away my phone and banished it. He wanted to know if my mom had told you anything."

"What? How can he do that? Nisha, you are giving him the power to do all this."

"I know. I have been so stupid and stubborn till now. But now I won't be so. I even stopped talking to my parents for him. I just don't get him at times. Sometimes he is so loving and caring and sometimes he is just the opposite."

"What will you do when you get back?"

"I will wait and watch for a month. If these people don't change, I will have to call off this marriage."

I sat and thought about my life. If Aryan had not supported me, my mother-in-law and sisters-in-law would have taken complete control of my life. Aryan was my power, my strength. I knew he would speak up for me any time. That is why I was not scared of anyone. Poor Nisha! Her husband never stood by her. Her pain was evident. It was not easy for her.

22

A Long Way

Nisha came back to India but nothing changed for her. In fact, things got worse. It had been months since she had seen her parents. Her sister-in-law still had a hold over everyone and everything. I just couldn't understand why she was so interested in interfering in her brother's life. And how stupid and blind Anuj was to listen to his sister.

Nisha never retaliated. She kept quiet in the hope that things would change but that did not happen.

Nisha's parents' health was deteriorating and I told Nisha to visit them.

I called Nisha at her parents' home.

"Hey, how are you? Happy at home?"

"Yes. My parents seem happier."

"Of course they are! Please eat well. Gain some weight."

"Yeah! Hey Alisha, I want to tell you something. These people have done a strange thing. Before I left, they gave me all my wedding jewellery."

"What? Then I am afraid they don't want you back."

"I thought so too. But what if I am wrong?"

"I don't know what to say. Those people are really weird."

"You know, I have been here for a week. But Anuj has called me just once. Whenever I call him, he never picks up the phone. My mother-in-law too hasn't picked up my calls."

"I guess it is obvious then."

I wished Nisha luck.

Nisha waited for two months. Then, she had enough. She went to her in-laws' place with her parents to find out what the matter was.

Instead of welcoming Nisha and her parents, Anuj reacted in an insane manner. He shouted at them for coming home without informing him. What could they do when he didn't answer their calls? Anuj insulted Nisha's parents and blamed Nisha for his misbehaviour towards them. Nisha could not tolerate him insulting her parents. She shouted at him. Then she left the house with her parents. She finally took the step she should have taken long ago. She lodged a complaint in the police station and filed for divorce. Her in-laws made deceitful allegations against her but Nisha fought back bravely.

Nisha was hurt. She couldn't believe Anuj would behave so cruelly. Before marriage, he had been so romantic and loving.

Time passed. Nisha felt better. She moved on. We girlfriends were really relieved.

Nisha applied for a job in a multi-national firm. She got the job and started working in Gurgaon.

Time passed. One day, we girls decided to meet up. It had been a long time. We needed to see each other.

We met for lunch at Kinbuck 2 in Connaught Place. We ordered some vodka and smoked from a *hookah.*

"My divorce would be final by next month," said Nisha.

"Great! You can find a great guy at my wedding," said Maria.

"What?" asked Ishika.

"Yes, I am getting married next month. Raj's parents have agreed; they even apologised. Finally, our love has won."

"Wow! Great! Cheers!"

We cheered together.

"Wish Maria a very happy married life," I said.

We cheered again.

"Girls, even I may get married soon. My parents are looking at a few profiles," said Ishika

"Yay! One more wedding party!" said Nisha.

"Guess what? There is a wedding at my house too! My younger sister-in-law's. We barely know each other but we will all be together for some time before the wedding. It is going to be fun shopping and making the wedding arrangements," I said.

"Great! The wedding season is on. Wish you all the very best," said Nisha.

"Looking at you people, I know life after marriage is not going to be that easy. I also guess it is a matter of luck what kind of people you end up with, whether it is a love marriage or an arranged one. Girls, I tell you seriously, I am a bit scared. At least you people knew your men before the wedding. I may not get that lucky. I don't know whom I will end up with. I hope I have accumulated some good *karma* in the past," said Ishika. She was on a high.

I said, "You may be right to an extent. It does not matter whether it is a love marriage or an arranged marriage. Both husband and wife have to work on their marriage to sustain it. Life is indeed beautiful after marriage. It's just that it takes some time to adjust with new people. It is not easy. We treat them like our parents and we expect them to treat us like their daughter. But that is not always the case. Their daughters get all the freedom but it is not given to us all the time. It all boils down to how you handle the situation. Marriage is all about giving and taking. Yes, Nisha's case was an exception. Maybe things will change with time. Nisha has good education and a career and no one can take that away from her. She will move on and find a better man."

"What about my case then? People are still prejudiced. Stereotypes still exist. Our society is full of hypocrites. You cannot change them. They are made this way. They may be dark but they want a fair daughter-in-law. We will always remain a daughter-in-law. We can never become their daughters," said Maria.

"Yes but atleast Raj is with you…that is what matters the most,"I said.

I knew Maria was quite right but I didn't want to argue and discourage Ishika. Marriage has its flaws but there are many positives too. A good marriage depends on the love and support of your partner, it's just that the other people should leave us alone and not interfere.

"I wish a nice guy comes into my life someday," said Nisha.

Nisha was seeing a therapist and she was feeling positive. I was happy for her.

"It is nice to see you talk positively. We finally have our old Nisha back," I said.

"Cheers for our darling Nisha," said Ishika.

We cheered… 'Yay…'

"We have come a long way," said Nisha.

"And we will go a long way," I said.

Glosssary

HENNA : A reddish brown dye, made from the powdered leaves of a tropical shrub, used to decorate the hands and legs, especially on weddings.

NAVRATRAS : A Hindu festival of fasting for nine days.

GAJRA : A flower garland women wear on their hair.

BARAAT : The groom's wedding party.

HALDI : turmeric mixed with curd that is applied on Indian brides before the wedding; it is believed to add a glow to their faces.

HALWA : An Indian Sweet dish.

SABZI : Vegetable.

SINDOOR : Red pigment made from powdered red lead, especially applied as a dot on the forehead or in the parting of the hair of married Hindu women.

BINDI : A decorative mark worn in the middle of the forehead by Indian woman, especially hindus.

POOJA : Prayer.